The Book Monster

An Ivy and Mack story

Written by Rebecca Colby
Illustrated by Gustavo Mazali

Collins

What's in this story?
Listen and say

shelf

floor

Download the audio at www.collins.co.uk/839775

read

Ivy comes home. Mack is reading.

4

Mack says, "Hello, Ivy."

Ivy says, "Why are you in my bedroom, Mack?"

Ivy says, "And why are my books on the floor?"

7

Ivy says, "Please put my books on my shelf, Mack."

Mack says, "Yes, the Book Monster put the books on the floor."

Ivy asks, "Where is the
Book Monster, Mack?"

Mack says, "I don't know. Croc and I can help put the books on the shelf."

Mack says, "Can you read a book to us, please?"

Ivy says, "Ok, one book."

Mack says, "This story, please ... with the alien."

Ivy says, "It's a very funny alien."

Ivy finishes the book.

Mack likes the story with the man on a horse. The man lives in the forest.

Ivy likes the story with the monkey.
It eats lots of bananas.

Now Mack has a story with a monster.
The monster likes singing.

Oh no! Look at the floor!

Picture dictionary

Listen and repeat

alien

forest

horse

monkey

monster

shelf

1 Look and order the story

2 Listen and say

Collins

Published by Collins
An imprint of HarperCollins*Publishers*
Westerhill Road
Bishopbriggs
Glasgow
G64 2QT

HarperCollins*Publishers*
1st Floor, Watermarque Building
Ringsend Road
Dublin 4
Ireland

William Collins' dream of knowledge for all began with the publication of his first book in 1819.

A self-educated mill worker, he not only enriched millions of lives, but also founded a flourishing publishing house. Today, staying true to this spirit, Collins books are packed with inspiration, innovation and practical expertise. They place you at the centre of a world of possibility and give you exactly what you need to explore it.

© HarperCollins*Publishers* Limited 2020

10 9 8 7 6 5 4 3 2

ISBN 978-0-00-839775-3

Collins® and COBUILD® are registered trademarks of HarperCollins*Publishers* Limited

www.collins.co.uk/elt

British Library Cataloguing in Publication Data

A catalogue record for this publication is available from the British Library.

Author: Rebecca Colby
Illustrator: Gustavo Mazali (Beehive)
Series editor: Rebecca Adlard
Publishing manager: Lisa Todd
Product managers: Jennifer Hall and Caroline Green
In-house editor: Alma Puts Keren
Project manager: Emily Hooton
Editor: Deborah Friedland
Proofreaders: Natalie Murray and Michael Lamb
Cover designer: Kevin Robbins
Typesetter: 2Hoots Publishing Services Ltd
Audio produced by id audio, London
Reading guide author: Julie Penn
Production controller: Rachel Weaver
Printed and bound by: GPS Group, Slovenia

Download the audio for this book and a reading guide for parents and teachers at www.collins.co.uk/839775